Forward

There is no prologue so you might at well read the forward. I always skipped it myself. I just felt the need to share what happened to me when I got invited to join a very unique fraternity. So I told my story to Stefan Pride an up and coming young author who has real potential. Too bad there won't be many people left to read his works. What does that mean you may think. Well read the book. If you like it recommend it to your more liberal minded friends. If you don't like it at least you have something in your archive and you've only blown a couple of bucks. If you enjoy it though, please let Stefan know. He could use the compliments. He has been depressed and a little jealous ever since I told him my story.

Enjoy your time. It is precious and short.

Jeff

My Strange Night

DEDICATIONS

I want to dedicate this short story to the people I love. Out of respect for them, I have elected not to mention their names. You know who you are. I also want to thank my twelfth grade English teacher for inspiring me to follow my dream and become a writer. She felt that with technology my spelling could be corrected and my syntactic structure could be artificially constructed as to be understandable. So thank you Barbara S. for all the criticism and support in helping me realize my dream. I'm sure that she is proud of my effort but is no doubt spinning in her grave over this story's content.

I also want to apologize to the football team for all the afternoons they spent in detention. I am sure they understand why I had to deny the stories they spread about what I did for them in the locker room on victory nights. I know some of them will be adding this book to their gay erotica collection. So guys extend my heartfelt regrets to the straight guys on our team. GO TEDDIES!

STRANGE FRAT LOVE
Or
HOW JEFF FOUND HIMSELF ALIENATED
Another work your mother neglected to warn you
about
by
STEFAN PRIDE

Just the fact I had been asked to join Omega Omega Omega was overwhelming for me. I had actually tried to network my way in to a few of the other fraternities on campus. But I had opted out of even trying to get in to the very elite Omega Omega Omega house. It had the reputation of being extremely unique among fraternities. Not only were all the members successful jocks, they represented the cream of every sport at my old and prestigious university. More than that they had all graduated at the top of their high school class. From what I understood they also came from all walks of life. Many came from very rich families, some from political clans, and some from blue-collar families, and some from European nobility. Regardless of their varied backgrounds all came from families that contributed in some way to the betterment of mankind. Also, not that I would notice this kind of thing but every guy in Omega Omega Omega was an absolute hunk!

No way in hell I would ever fit in this group. I'm not much of a jock unless that means keeping your body toned by regular visits to the gym. I didn't graduate at the top of my class but I did well enough to get a full scholarship to an Ivy League college on the east coast. My family background, I don't know. A middle class couple that adopted me, after a drunk driver killed my parents raised me. I really don't remember much about my real parents except my mother was soft and always smelled good, but was seldom ever home it seemed. My father and his brother were always taking me places that were fun. He would snuggle up with me in bed and read a story to me before I fell off to sleep. I liked those times. I remember his smile and his laugh. He had very blonde hair just like I do. After the accident I never saw my uncle again, I apparently had no other relatives, at least no one who cared enough to take me. I was fortunate to have great adoptive parents. My adopted dad is an attorney with a decent practice in our little Midwest town. My mom had been a schoolteacher until they got me. They were an older couple that had given up on ever having children. I was just like a real son to them and I think I've made them proud. So I have no complaints. Every thing considered life was treating me well. But an invitation to be considered for membership to Omega Omega Omega! Awesome!

The invitation had said to be there at eight Saturday evening in dressy casual attire. Since no one I was aware of had been invited and I didn't have a car I knew I would have to walk. It was a nice brisk October evening, so the two-mile walk from my dorm to the fraternity house was actually quite pleasant. I walked past one regal Victorian house after the next. These stately homes were not unusual in this old prosperous university town. These houses built so closely together ended suddenly when I got to the block of my destination. Here began a magnificent forested park area that appeared to be completely enclosed by a granite block wall about four feet tall and two feet thick additionally it was topped by a wrought iron fence, which I guessed to be about seven feet in height. About fifty feet beyond this corner was a set of magnificent gates. The bulk of the gates were fashioned from wrought iron, but huge dragons fashioned of brass centered each gate. At the entrance were two men dressed in security type uniforms stopping each car and verifying the invitations with photo ID's. The cars varied from expensive little sports cars, plush sedans, to a black stretch limo and even the occasional student four cylinder. As I approached on foot, the guards looked at me curiously. The invitation along with my picture identification seemed to satisfy them and they signaled me through the gates. The driveway was wide and curved around to the right. It was bordered on both sides by huge trees in full fall color. Brown, orange, red, and multicolor leaves were falling everywhere and the cool air smelled of change. The house was nowhere in sight so I just kept walking. The house has to be here somewhere.

I heard the muffled purr of an engine approaching me from behind. I looked back to make sure I was out of the way. Approaching me was a sleek silver Bentley convertible, its black top closed of course due to the temperature. It was the kind of car I had only read about, we certainly didn't see these in Middletown, Ohio. The car came to a stop when the front passenger door was right next to me. The window silently lowered revealing the very handsome smiling face of a black haired man whom I guessed to be in his mid twenties.

"Hello Jeff. The house is about quarter of a mile further. Hop in the back and we will give you a ride the rest of the way." How did he know my name?

"Gee Sir, thanks! I really appreciate it." I slid in to the back seat. The interior of the car had the very masculine scent of new leather. Sitting next to the handsome man driving the car was the most incredibly beautiful young man I had ever seen. He was about my age with a head full of the most extravagantly lustrous ebony hair, feathered down to his shoulders.

"Jeff this is my son Paxton." Paxton's smile sparkled and was both easy and sincere. How can a man that young have a son that old, I thought.

"It's my pleasure to finally meet you Jeff. As president of Omega Omega Omega , I can speak for all the brothers that we are happy you decided to accept our invitation." Paxton said to me in a warm but very well bred tone. What incredible purple eyes he had, as did his father. I had never seen eyes like that. Except for my own!

I was really starting to get nervous about this whole thing. This entire situation struck me as being weird. Why had I been invited to this place? How did someone I had never met before know my name? What about the eyes?

"Look what's this all about? Pardon my midwestern curiosity but you pulling over and knowing who I am is freaky. I want to know what this is all ...." My words stopped flowing as the most magnificent mansion I had ever seen came into view. The palatial mansion consisted of four floors of granite with what had to be three dozen floor to ceiling windows on each floor and each ablaze with light. The luxury car pulled under a great portico where liveried valets opened our three doors simultaneously.

"Welcome back Mr. Vanderseer." Well now at least I knew his name, a detail that had been passed over in our initial introduction. Then it dawned on me that on our campus there were numerous buildings that bore that name. There was Vanderseer Medical Arts, Vanderseer Science Building, Vanderseer Theater of Arts, and those were just the ones I was familiar with. Most importantly I was a student here under a full Vanderseer scholarship fund! I had been just on the verge of being a smartass with my college future! Mr. Vanderseer smiled when he saw my epiphany.

"It is of no consequence Jeff. The Vandeseer family merely gives back to the university that has given us so much over the generations." That beautiful warm smile again set me right at ease. "I'm sure that Paxton will have most if not all of your questions answered by the end of tonight's "recruitment" party." That was the end of that conversation.

Paxton walked up behind me and in his best president of Omega Omega Omega voice said, "Come on Jeff. I know all of this must seem mysterious, but it will all make sense to you. I will be disappointed if it does not. Now let me introduce you to your future brothers. First, though, let's get a drink in hand. Remember, anything you want just ask for it or get it yourself. This, hopefully, will be where you live for the next four years and your home forever."

Strange words I thought. But after the walk here I decided I needed a beer. Paxton handed me an import I had never had before and he elected to have a crystal flute of champagne. Hell, I had rarely ever had a sip of lager back in Middletown let alone an import or champagne.

Paxton didn't really have to take me around introducing me. No more had we walked away from the mahogany bar than one after another of the room's young men were surrounding us, shaking my hand and using my first name before being told what it was. There were other students in the room that seemed to be in my situation. That is, under scrutiny. I decided to ignore the fact that all of us had either blonde hair or lustrous black hair and everyone had my purple eyes. Maybe that's their criteria l laughed to myself.

When there was a lull in introductions I asked Paxton, who had not left my side, "How many of us are you considering for brotherhood?"

"Well, there are thirty-two here. But only twenty will be chosen by morning." Paxton answered briefly. "Ah look father is about to address the room."

Mr. Vanderseer had stepped up on a stage that ran across one end of the magnificent room, which I was later to learn was called the men's parlor. It really looked more like a baronial banquet hall than a parlor.

"Welcome gentlemen! Greetings fellow brothers! We are here tonight as we are the second Saturday of every October and as we have been for two hundred years. We, the representative tribal fathers have gathered here from many parts of the world to oversee this year's selection of new brothers.

"What tribal fathers?" I asked Paxton.

He smiled and whispered, "They are in the next room. You will meet them later. First you will meet the women."

Well I was shocked. I hadn't seen a woman here.

"No more questions Jeff. You will see and hopefully like," Jeff smiled.

"To thirty-two of you the program is new", Mr. Vanderseer continued. "For the next ninety minutes, gentlemen, the Omega Omega Omega brother chosen as your escort will show you around our house so that you can become more familiar with your home. After that you will meet the ladies and be introduced to "the one." After that you will meet the fathers. With that I bid you adieu until later. Enjoy!" With those final words Mr. Vanderseer turned and exited through a door that wasn't even visible when shut.

I was trying to assimilate some of the speech. "Well alrighty then. I must confess to being somewhat confused, " I said looking at Paxton. "So who is my escort?"

"I am of course. I hope that meets with your approval." With that Paxton placed his hand on the small of my back and guided me back to the bar for refills and with glass in hand we headed out of the parlor and back into the grand foyer.

"This is the great and main entrance to the house." Explained Paxton in his best tour guide mode.

The room was huge; in fact my house in Middletown could almost fit in it. The floor was in smoky grey marble and the walls were various shades of the lightest hues of blue. Paxton explained that the entire mansion had been brought over from England just before the American Civil War. At the end of the foyer was the most magnificent horseshoe stairway. I guessed each side to be about ten feet wide and it maintained that width as it curved up to a balcony that was supported by great Doric columns of sapphire blue. The steps themselves were of flawlessly brilliant white marble. The focal point of the thirty-foot ceiling was a vast crystal chandelier that must have been aglow with a hundred candle-like lights. Paxton explained that we would go to the upper floors later, but first he wanted to show me the lower level. My very handsome escort led me to a large door at the end of the foyer, which led to another sizable stair.

"I think you will like this really a lot," enthused Paxton, losing some of his upper class tone and smiling like a little boy. (What was getting into me? I could barely keep my eyes off this cute jock. I hadn't dated much in high school but I knew I was into girls!).

Descending the stairway we found ourselves in an enormous room. To our left was a wall of mostly glass with three sets of French doors that if opened would lead to a great stone patio with sloping gardens beyond it. To our right was an Olympic size swimming pool that was more impressive than the one at the university. I stood staring in amazement.

"I thought you would like this. Swimming is one of my favorite things too." Paxton stated. How did he know I liked to swim?

"If you like, we can go swimming after the party. Come over here we are not finished yet." Paxton said as he took my hand (wait a minute he doesn't have to hold my hand. But I didn't pull it away) and led me to another door that opened up to a clay paved full tennis court.

"Wow!" was all I could think to say. "What did you say the dues were here?" I asked, knowing that I could never afford membership to this fraternity. "Look, this is all really incredible. But since you already knew my name and so much else about me, you must know that all this is way beyond my ability to pay. So why taunt me wi..."

"I said everything would be explained Jeff. " Interrupted Paxton. "Please just enjoy the tour and everything will come together. I promise."

Still holding my hand Paxton led me to a locker room that smelled of men and sweat. The muskiness of the locker room combined with the humidity coming from the shower room and Paxton holding my hand had given me an embarrassingly prominent erection. When he led me through yet another door that opened into a vast exercise equipment room outfitted with every imaginable machine for keeping in shape, he turned toward me and caught me adjusting my dick to a more comfortable discreet angle. He smiled.

"The smells from the locker room do that to me too." As proof he tightened the left leg of his pants and the outline of a thick tubular was evident going down his left thigh. He must wear boxers I thought. I also hoped that I didn't get a woody every time I went into the gym. It also crossed my mind that Paxton had something to do with it. I eyed his crotch a little too long for my own comfort, cleared my throat and totally changed the subject.

"This fitness room is amazing! There are machines here that will have to be explained or I might get tangled up in them!" I laughed thinking of the possibilities for mishap.

The wall in front of the double row of treadmills and stair steppers was covered from floor to ceiling with what I assumed were plasma TV screens. There must have been fifty I quickly guessed.

"Impressive isn't it?" asked Paxton. "Here while you exercise you can watch what is going on all over the world at any given moment. We have a satellite system so we are not limited to getting just the point of view of the USA. That way we can observe, digest, report, and make our own conclusions and recommendations to the Fathers. Also, literally every class at the university is recorded and downloaded here so that if our work ever makes it necessary to miss a class we can play catch up in a healthy way." Paxton explained as if all of this was normal.

"Paxton, I must tell you that this is not what I thought of when I got invited to live in a frat house. I thought of frat houses as fun party places with lots of girls to screw and kegs of beer. My father even warned me about them for the benefit of my mother. He belonged to one at his school in Ohio. He told me once when mom wasn't around that a fraternity is a place to screw your brains out, make life long friends, and get drunk, but to watch it because I was in a university to get a good education. I don't see that happening here. Not that I could afford it anyway. I think we should stop the tour here and let me thank you and not waste your time." I told Paxton in the most polite straightforward way I could.

Actually the picture my father painted of frat life did not really appeal to me the way I thought it should. I really wanted to study and learn. The thought of having to screw girls and get drunk to be popular really is not what I am about. At the same time I wanted both acceptance and popularity. I knew in my heart Omega Omega Omega was where I belonged from the minute I walked into the house. It just seemed like something that financially would be out of my reach.

"Jeff please you can't go! I've been waiting for you." Paxton stopped at that last statement and started to rephrase. "I mean I've been waiting to sponsor you ever since the committee submitted names for this year's pledges. I agree, ours is a different sort of fraternity, but I think you will like it here. If screwing girls is what you want there is no shortage of them trying to go with our members. As for getting drunk regularly, you can, but that wouldn't work out and I don't think you want too. We offer a whole new way of life to you. It will be explained. As for cost, the operational expenses of this house are phenomenal. But money is the least of your concerns I can assure you. Just please let me finish the tour before you make a decision."

Paxton was actually pleading with me. How could I turn down those eyes?

"Ok man, I'm not trying to be difficult or unappreciative. In fact I really like this place and I really like the thought of being your friend. So if you think I can afford it and you want some hick from Middletown Ohio in your group then lead the way Mr. President!" I laughed and patted his back. I would really like to pat his butt, I thought, but like I had since puberty, I quickly assigned that thought to a special closet in the back of my mind. I noticed my host stop for a fleeting second after that butt thought.

Paxton seemed really relieved and we left the lower level of the house and back to the main floor. We spoke to a few brothers, some of who had a potential member like myself in tow. We decided that my beer was too warm and Paxton's champagne had gotten stale so he went to one of the bars and quickly had them replaced with cold fresh drinks. Once again, taking my hand like it was the most normal thing in the world he led me to great horseshoe stairs and we ascended the steps on the right to the landing above. Hanging on the landing wall and looking over the balcony of the great entrance hall was one of the largest paintings I had ever seen outside a museum.

It was a portrait of a man I guessed to be thirty.

His attire was from the last half of the eighteenth century. He had long flowing blonde hair and was seated on the most beautiful white steed. His was surely the most handsome face to ever grace a canvas. He was posed so that he looked as if he were watching the activities of this grand mansion and his purple eyes were missing nothing.

"Who the hell is that? I asked mesmerized by a man long since dead.

"That my dear Jeff is Geoffrey Hanover and you are in "Hanover House". This house was dismantled in England in the 1850's and brought here shipload-by-shipload and reassembled here. There of course have been improvements made but essentially the house is original. " Paxton explained this with great pride.
"Now please follow me this way." Paxton said and walked ahead of me to the right. As he walked I couldn't help but look once again at what a great butt he had. I pictured him naked but just as quickly put his pants back on him. I thought I heard my host chuckle. What was coming over me? The hallway before us was, like everything else in this house, enormous and very long. There were electric torches protruding from the walls on each side and between each touchier were oil portraits of very handsome men dressed in garbs from various periods of time. All had either blonde hair like mine or jet black like Paxton, but they all possessed the purple eyes.

"Paxton are these members of the Hanover family or past brothers of Omega Omega Omega?" I asked.

"Your guess is right on both counts. Some are the direct descendants of Geoffrey Hanover but all of them are brothers. Many of their descendants are current students here and some of the descendants have been brought here tonight and offered membership."

Paxton was forever weirding me out with these kind of statements. I decided that he might be doing this just to see how I react, so I didn't react.

"I guess then, that a lot of these are former Vanderseers?" I looked at him raising my eyebrows.

"Guilty." Paxton said with a faked concern.

"Why me? Are you wanting to introduce some new blood to the group?" I asked with a lighthearted but very grandiose gesture toward myself.

"No, never new we have found that the old works great and when new is introduced it has historically backfired." I could tell Paxton being quite sincere.

Before Paxton could say anything I said with an exasperated voice, "I know, I know. It will be explained to me. On with the tour Mr. President."

"Well you have actually had as much of the tour as you are going to get for now. If you formally accept our offer of brotherhood you will become privy to the floor above this one which I really want to show you." Paxton informed me.

By this time we had walked all the way to the end of the hall and were standing by a door. Paxton placed his hand on the very large ornate brass doorknob.

"Come in here with me and we will talk. I will answer as many of your questions as I officially can. If you decide to proceed with the haze, after what is offered you in this room, the Fathers will answer the rest of your questions. Do you wish to go in there?" The president of this strange fraternity asked me.

"Haze? What are you talking about now? What is the room? And why are "the Fathers" involved in this membership?" I demanded feeling both nervous and irritated at once.

Irritated because I was still erect and was afraid that at any moment my khaki dress pants were going to start showing a big wet spot right below my belt. Why didn't I wear sensible dark pants like Paxton so that semen wouldn't show, I wondered. Then I wondered why I even thought of that. This was truly the strangest night of my life so far. If only I had known!

"You look fine in the khaki pants, believe me." Paxton said smiling.

Ok this was too weird! I had thought that thought not verbalized it. Paxton ignored my near look of panic.

"I said Haze because this whole evening has been a haze of sorts. Every door in this hallway leads to a bedroom suite. This one is mine and has been for the two years I have lived here. It will hopefully be our room as it was planned to be. The Fathers are involved in your membership because one of the purposes of their life is to keep this fraternity alive as a brotherhood and off the grid to those who would destroy us, and society along with us."

"I know it sounds like I have a really limited vocabulary, but this is very freaky. I repeat very fucking freaky! But I've gone this far and the curious side of me has got to find out what makes you very strange people tick." With that decision made I walked past Paxton and into the bedroom.

The room did not look like the frat boy's room that would have come to mind just a few hours ago with all the mahogany on the walls and rich tufted leather furniture. It was quite sizable with a wall of bookcases filled with leather bound volumes, two large desks with computers, a mini fridge and micro. Being a corner room it had six large windows with two of them being doors that looked like they led to a balcony. The large stressed leather couch and chairs were grouped in front of a large fireplace with a wood fire crackling in it. Paxton showed me a closet, which I assumed to be his, that held more clothes than I had owned over my lifetime. It was a walk through closet with a dressing room that opened into a bathroom with a huge shower and double sink. On one side of the sink were all the things a man needed for proper hygiene. I assumed these were Paxton's also. On the other side there was a toothbrush, toothpaste, mouthwash, hairbrush, and deodorant, which looked familiar. Out of curiosity I walked back to the dressing room/closet and opened one of the doors opposite Paxton's. There on about six hangers were my jeans and shirts. I found my underwear and t-shirts along with my socks in some drawers.

"I assumed you would be accepting. Some of the others…actually all the others thought I was being premature. Please don't be angry. " Paxton implored me.

I was somewhat beyond angry but I was more scared I think than anything. I didn't say anything, but brushed past Paxton and went back into the main room and looked at what must have been a king size bed.

"If we are supposed to be sharing this room where is my bed?" I asked just to see what he would say. The answer was becoming all too clear.

"Jeff that is your bed. You have a left side preference. If you look in the nightstand you will find your book that you read before sleeping. I am a right side preference. It is my bed too. But I am hoping that you will sleep towards the middle. That is what I tend to do."

"Paxton I know I'm a little naïve and certainly not very worldly, but isn't it a little strange for college kids even in a fraternity to sleep in the same bed?" It was really meant to be a rhetorical question but I couldn't seem to throw Paxton.
"In most fraternity houses probably. But there are some of the more liberal colleges that have that kind of set up. " Paxton walked to within a foot of me and placing his hands on my shoulders looked me straight in the eye with those sparkling purple orbs. "Jeff just give this a chance. I love you and have since I first saw a video of you five years ago. I also think you love me. You just haven't come to that realization yet." He told me this looking me in the eyes and I heard him but his lips weren't moving.

I thought about bolting for the door. But I just stood there with my mouth open and...I still had a fucking hardon. My cock staining the front of my pants should be my last concern I thought.

"Please Jeff don't bolt and for what it's worth my dick is still hard too." Paxton shot the thought into my head. "Don't be scared. You can talk to me too without sound. Try it. It will get more and more natural for you."

"Are the other thirty-one guys going through this or is it just me?" I thought to him.

"Yes, but remember I told you there were only twenty. The other twelve have already been sent home. If a sponsoring brother felt that a "potential" would not fit in with us, then he was never invited into the sponsor's bedroom. Instead he was walked to the door and told we would let him know and he was sent home. It was pretty much known before tonight who would not make it. However, with something as important as this it is important to confirm our decision. He will receive a polite letter of rejection along with a tuition scholarship from the Hanover Foundation. He will go through college and beyond. Eventually he will contribute to society and perhaps even take an illustrious place in history. Those that are asked to stay are the true luminaries. But we all fill a critical need."

I liked this talking mind to mind. Then it dawned on me and I am sure I turned red as a beet.

"Then you heard me take your pants off so I could see what your butt must look like?" I thought to Paxton hoping he would tell me he had not been aware of that thought but at the same time realizing that my question just told him if he didn't already know. This time the laughter was audible and he shook his head yes and kept laughing. Suddenly I was laughing too.

"I was flattered, however." He assured me in his deep rich voice. Suddenly the laughter stopped and he was looking at me seriously.

"I was hoping that this would move faster, but you kept asking so many damn questions that now I'm behind schedule. So hoping you will forgive me I want to make love with you." He told me very simply glancing at his watch. "All the others are way beyond where we are. But your case is a little more complicated when your background is taken into consideration."

With those words Paxton drew my face to his and gave me the longest softest hardest wet kiss I had ever had (Not that I had ever had a wet kiss and certainly not from a boy). As I tried to suck in my breath in both surprise and need of air I got his tongue exploring my mouth instead.

"I know already! I thought to him. "You will explain later. Right?"

"Right." He shot back to me.

I had actually never made love to a woman (I had heard gossip about some of the easy girls in my high school, but the few girls I dated slapped my hand if it grazed their breast at a movie) and certainly not to a man (In fact I had never even done the popular circle jerk that I heard some of my jock friends whisper about). But I decided to make my first time as enjoyable as I could, since it didn't look like my heterosexual instincts were going to come to the fro and defend me. We kissed for what seemed liked a short eternity before Paxton broke it. He actually stopped the kiss before I wanted him to. His next move made me forget wanting the kiss as he bent his head and brought those luscious lips to the nape of my neck and licked and sucked on my skin. For a blonde, I have a heavy beard and Paxton seemed to really enjoy licking the stubble along my jaw.

With surprisingly inexperienced hands, he was unbuttoning my shirt and pulling it from my pants. I was just standing there like an idiot doing nothing in return while Paxton kept kissing and licking me lower on my chest and nipping at my nipples which immediately went erect and sent electrifying jolts of pleasure to my brain. He raised each arm up just enough to bury his nose and lips into my pits.

I thought if I died right this minute I would leave this earth with no regrets. While thinking this I noticed that Paxton was now on his knees in front of me. He was unzipping my pants! This was a really fast dive for me into this new lifestyle. Then I added a "Don't you think so?" mental flash to Paxton since I didn't seem to have any private thoughts anyway.

"Fast but not unprecedented." He thought back to me. "Your thoughts will be private from the other brothers but for the most part not from me. At least not for a while but as you develop you will be able to keep some things from me. After a relatively short time you will start to have a 'bi-mind' as will I. That is, even if we are on opposite sides of the world we will hear each other think and help each other find solutions to whatever. That process will start after we mate and grow stronger each time we make love. Now enough with the explanations! You have no idea how long I have anticipated putting this cock into my mouth." He smiled at me as he fished my rigid manhood through my now open zipper.

Without any hesitation Paxton slid his lips over the head of my cock and soon the entire shaft was sleeved in moist warmth. I thought it impressive how he took
my thick seven and three quarter inch (which I had

measured regularly and hopefully it still had a ways to grow) pride down his throat until my very blonde curly pubes were tickling at his nose. Slowly he applied suction and pulled back up until he could feather tickle around the rim of my crown. Then he started repeating the process faster and faster. I am young and orgasm was building up fast. I was about to blow and it was going to be a major wad. It had been at least a week since I jacked off. My roommate or one of his friends was always in the dorm so I had little opportunity.

"No my sweet. Don't come yet." Paxton whispered in my mind and suddenly he quit sucking me.

"Why did you stop? I would have told you before I came so you could pull off." I said very audibly. Laughing Paxton said there is more we have to do and we have a schedule. Jeez! I thought. This is my first sex, involving another person, even if it is queer and I'm on a fucking time line! Paxton just looked at me, smiled and shook his head.

It was then I realized that my pleasure giver was still in his suit and tie and I was standing there with no shirt and my cock sticking out from my zipper and leaking like a sieve.

"Don't worry Jeff I'm going to take care of that. Let me help you slip your pants off. I would not be offended, by the way, if you helped me get out of my clothes." Paxton said in a hopeful voice.

"Well I guess," was all I said, feigning boredom.

No sooner were my pants and briefs off than I was busy helping my new friend out of his Armani jacket, sliding that tie off, and unbuttoning his Valentino shirt. (I think he is a designer nut.)

"Jeff please don't kill the mood." I heard in my head.

Damn this is going to get annoying until I can block some of it, I was thinking as I slid off his shoes and pulled down his pants and boxers in one fast but gentle jerk. Before me was what must have been a beautiful cock. I didn't have much to compare it with but it was bigger in girth than mine and had me by at least an inch. He had the face of a boy, but this huge dick with its large veins twisting up from its root was definitely a man's. Not to mention the muscles of his smooth thighs. Possibly a refined rich snob, but muscles like his are earned.

"Thank you Jeff, except for the snob part." Came the thought.

"Damn!" I thought back.

"Well now what?" I asked in my real voice.

"Now I want you to lay back on the bed and let me get to know you. Remember, I haven't done this before either." Except for the initial inexperienced hands, how could Paxton expect me to believe that after the demo he had just given me?"

Sorry babe. But that is the truth. I have to take the complete lead in this because of your circumstances. Don't ask me what that means, you will find out," Paxton said and I knew he was speaking the truth. Now I was lying in the center of the huge bed. Paxton was standing at the foot of the bed gazing down at me with what I knew was true love and possibly a little lust thrown in. How could that happen in less than two hours? I don't know. That is just how it was turning out. I was gazing back at him. How could anything this beautiful be in love with me? He had such extraordinary features that he almost didn't look real. The jet-black hair hanging to his shoulders with a few strands out of place and covering some of his left eye, gave him kind of a messy little boy look. His skin was so pale that the contrast with his raven dark hair was surreal. He had no hair on his chest, legs, or arms. There was a generous tuft sticking out slightly from each armpit. His balls hung low and appeared huge but they too were hairless. Only the thatch around his cock hair that was luxuriant, shiny, and not trimmed. I couldn't help but lick my lips. He smiled and thought to me that he had not trimmed his cock hair like the other guys were always doing because he had learned I was fascinated by a lot of hair there. I had not consciously known this myself but now realized what he said was correct. I accepted his explanation with a smile.

Paxton crawled catlike onto the bed, looking at me, and smiling all the while. He reached for my right foot and raised it up, looked at me, and lowered his mouth. He placed each of my toes in turn into his mouth and licked and sucked them and did the same with the other foot. I had never felt anything so good. My cock could not possibly get any harder I thought as I watched it expand some more. My feet licked and sucked clean, Paxton began advancing up my leg each one in turn.

Now, my legs, unlike his, are covered in almost white blonde hair that is hard to see from a distance but I knew by the sounds emanating from Paxton's throat that he liked hairy legs. His tongue played with and curled the hair on my thigh, which made him laugh with delight. He slowly flipped me over onto my stomach and I felt him nuzzling my crack and using his hands to pull it open wide. As soon as he did this I felt a shot of ecstasy ripple through me and I very audibly moaned my approval and shock as I felt what had to be his tongue enter my asshole. He licked and sucked and fucked my hole for at least ten minutes. I would have been content if he had never stopped. Just a short while ago I would have called someone a liar if they told me that people did that and that it felt good. This was quite a night!

When Paxton had his fill, he urged me back on my back where I must have had a really silly grin on my face. He said to enjoy it because I would certainly be given the opportunity to return the favor. Due to the schedule it might not happen tonight but it would happen. We'll see, I thought.

"Oh don't worry you will" formed the thought in my head.

Now once again on my back Paxton lowered his whole body on mine. I could feel his cock twitching against my twitch, which felt really good. He had my leg hair smashed down with his smooth body. I heard him think how good the bristle tickle felt and how fantastic my smooth chest felt against his. Then he opened his mouth just as I opened mine and we were once again kissing like we would never see each other again. Paxton was literally fucking my mouth with his tongue. With every thrust in, our tongues would duel for position. Then just like with sucking my dick he stopped the kiss.

"Damn I wish you would quit doing that!" I told him.

"Schedule." He responded. "It's because of…"

"I know. Because of my special circumstances." I finished the sentence for him. He laughed.

"Are you going to be so petulant for the rest of our lives?"

"Probably. Why do you ask?" He ignored me.

"The time has come. What we have been doing is better than even I imagined." Paxton whispered to me. "But I am told that what comes next will be all that you felt, and more. Eventually these won't be necessary for us, but in keeping with the times as it were." Paxton said as he reached over to his nightstand and grabbed a bottle and a packet. It was of course a rubber and the bottle was lube. Both were new to me.

Some of my friends and I used to joke about buying a condom to carry in case we ever needed it, but we never really had the need. Or at least I didn't.

"What the fuck is that for?" I stupidly asked.

"Precisely." Stated Jeff. "You my love are going to fuck me and I'm going to teach you how. But be gentle because I will also be fucking you with your permission." Why, I thought did we have to do this now? Think schedule Jeff came the thought.

" Whatever." I answered to no one in particular.

Just like an old pro Paxton tore open the condom, placed a little lube on the inside and slid it down my dick. It was a tight fit but it didn't feel bad. He then proceeded to put a lot of lube on my cockshaft getting the condom nice and slick. He poured even more into his hand and reached behind himself and applied it to his hole. He maneuvered himself so that he was on all fours.

"This should be the best way for my first penetration. You need to get behind me and massage my hole with your finger to get it relaxed and then start working your cockhead in me. I will concentrate on pushing out. Get the head of the cock in as quickly as you can and then just stop until my anus adjusts to your presence and size. I will tell you when to push in further. You got it?" He sounded like he was quoting an instruction manual.

"I think so. Let me know if I am hurting you. The timeframe for whatever reason can be stopped." I assured him as I got up on my knees behind him.
I had never been this close to a boy's ass before and here I was looking for his shit hole to stick my virgin cock into. What a night!

It wasn't too hard to find. It turned out to be a cute little pink starfish looking thing. I dabbed some of the lube on my index finger and stuck it tentatively in the hole. I got up to one joint and felt the amazing warmth and tightness. I moved it around and pushed in a little further. I heard Paxton suck in a quick breath.

"Push it in further and work it back and forth," he told me. "Now put in another finger with it." I did as the inside voice told me.

"Bend the finger about an inch past the muscle ring and you will feel a hard little nut like thing. Rub against it." Fuck I had never heard this voice before or maybe I had but it wasn't Paxton. Great I thought I got a party line going on in my head. But I did as instructed, found the little nodule and rubbed it.

"Oh fuck!" yelled Paxton with all the upper class tone gone from his voice. "That feels absolutely incredible. Where did you learn that?"

"I'll explain it to you later," I shot back at him.

"Oh Jeff! Just take your fucking finger out of my ass and stick your cock in me. Now!" Yelled Paxton.

I kind of wondered if pressing on that little nodule was like pressing on an obscenity button. Oh well. Always one to serve my fellow man I did what Paxton asked I withdrew my fingers and stuck the head of my cock in his tight orifice.

"Stop. Stop! Motherfucker that hurts! Just stay where you are Jeff. Let me get used to that thick dick of yours." Well, all of Paxton's refinery was out the window. I waited a moment.

"You ready Pax? I've got to push that son of a bitch in deeper. It feels so fucking good!" I guess my Bible belt upbringing had gone out the window too.

"Go for it babe. I'm ready as I will ever be." With that Paxton pushed back toward me and before I knew it I was cock hair deep in that tight pale ass.

We started the fucking motion and I was really getting into it. Never had I felt such an all-encompassing sensation. The moist white-hot canal was generating pleasure beyond description. As I moved my engorged penis back and forth I couldn't believe the slick tightness. With just a half inch thrust forward each one of the thousands of nerve endings in my cock's head fired a wave of ecstasy. I couldn't get enough. I starting pumping like a schoolboy rushing a jack off session so he doesn't get caught. I knew in that moment that this would not be the last time I fucked a man.

"Stop baby boy," a moaning Paxton ordered.

"What the fuck! Not again", I thought as Paxton pulled several inches forward so that my cock came out of his ass with a wet plopping sound.

There I was with my staff just sticking straight out and in my mind's eye looking lost and confused. He told me inside my head not to worry, my cock would be back where it had established rights soon enough. With that thought (literally) Paxton turned over on his back and pulled his knees to his chest with his feet spaced well apart.

"Move forward so that my ankles are at each of your shoulders. I understand re-entry will not be the issue that initial penetration was and will, in fact, be quite satisfying for me as well."

What was Paxton doing? Quoting from a sex book he had memorized? As much as I was enjoying the pure lust of our sex, I was hoping for a little intimacy and romance with my first time. Even if my first time was with a guy, I thought.

"Later Jeff, I promise. I am a romantic too. The important thing is that we get linked. And there is the schedule." Paxton projected to me but gave a very audible grunt as my glistening cockhead breached that tight pink hole.

I was still sitting up on my knees, much like I did when taking communion at the Episcopal Church back in Middletown. This was so much better than religion. I slowly pushed my staff all the way in. I could no longer see my root. Paxton's balls were pulled up tight in his scrotum, which was resting on my cock. I let the shaft rest deep inside him. I had a thousand thoughts going through my head. How had I ended up here in this luxurious room having sex with a man? If only my parents and friends back home knew what I was doing? What about my expected future of being an engineer with a wife and one point six children? These thoughts all happened in a fraction of a second and then dissolved as I was once again focusing on the warmth around my cock. I thought what a completely beautiful contrast the raven blackness of his pubic hair was to my almost platinum blonde dick hair. The hair almost looked like they were stretching toward each other and intertwining. I looked up at Paxton and his smile was big and very loving. I smiled back and deep purple eyes stared into deep purple eyes.

Paxton reached toward me and placed his hands on my shoulders pulling down and toward him. His muscled legs moved behind my ass and locked around me.

"Move forward Jeff. You are not so heavy as to cause discomfort. Put your lips together and move in him. He loves the feel of your thigh hair tickling his thighs." That familiar voice in my head again.

I did as advised. It was even more of a turn on watching Paxton's eyes as I fucked him. My tempo picked up. Paxton was yelling for me to fuck him harder. I hope no one is outside the door or in the next room for that matter, I thought.

"Please come in me Jeff. I want to feel you spasm in my ass. I want to hear the sounds of your orgasm in my ears not my head when you blast in me. Faster! Faster Jeff!" The very proper Paxton was as involved as I, and by his grunting and cussing even more so.

"Oh fucking yes Paxton! I'm going to cum. I am going to cum any sec...Ahhhh! Ahhhh! Fuck! I'm shooting it in your ass!" I was shouting.

My legs had gone tense and my whole being was concentrating on seeding this manboy that I had met such a short time ago. Just as suddenly, the jolts of pure ecstasy gave way to waves of body wide pleasure and then began subsiding. I lay there. Our eyes had never lost contact. Paxton's hands were still on my back and my dick still lodged deep in him. It wasn't softening. I was ready to go again.

"Paxton can I please do it again? Like now?" I said to him, like a little boy wanting to stay on the roller coaster.

"Later. I promise you can keep that thing in me as often as you like. But right now we need to turn the tables." Paxton's eyes sparkled.

"Ok babe. Whatever you say. What do want to do now?"

"I just told you Jeff. Turn the tables. I need to fuck you."

I'm sure the smile vanished from my face and my mouth must have dropped open. Paxton was considerably bigger than me and I had never even had a thermometer in my butt before.

"Paxton I really need to study. I think I should be going home. Long walk and all." This time Paxton lost the smile.

"HaHa! I got one over on the smartass mind reader!" I laughed and Paxton looked slightly annoyed. "That big cock of yours is going to hurt like hell. But Paxton, I've never wanted anything so badly in my life as having that huge tube of yours fucking me."

Because of the mysterious "timeframe," things moved very quickly. Paxton wasted no time lubing his fingers and introducing them in my asshole just as he had me do earlier. With three of his long narrow fingers wiggling in my ass, there was some discomfort. I was getting scared I must admit. Then I resolved to make the most of this. If Paxton could take my prick like a man I figured I could do this high toned Ivy Leaguer one better. I was positioned on my back and to take the edge off as he finger fucked me, he very expertly licked my twitching cock, lapping the leakage from my slit every few seconds. He thought to me to flip over on my stomach and get on all fours.

"No Pax I want to stay on my back so I can watch you. I don't want to miss watching you for any of this."

"It will really be much more uncomfortable the first time if you do it that way." Paxton told me with genuine concern in his voice.

"It will hurt at first no matter what. I've made my decision. Now fuck me!"

He used so much lube it was almost overkill but a sweet gesture. I know my hole was twitching with anticipation as Paxton very carefully touched it with the head of his long thick cock. He had his entire right hand wrapped around his dick. I noticed, uneasily, that his thumb and fingers didn't quite meet. He did little circle motions of his dick around my rosebud in an effort to relax me. There was little chance of that happening. He finally placed the latex covered staff directly against my entrance and pushed maybe half an inch of the huge tip in me. I sucked in a quick breath and he stopped, not pulling out.

"Are you ok Jeff?" He shot the question through my head. He barely had anything in me and I could feel the intense burn as the muscle ring resisted the reverse pressure.

"Push out Jeff. Just like you are trying to eliminate. You won't, so don't worry. Just push out and entry will be less of an effort." The voice said in my head. Paxton saw me grit my teeth and I probably had a grimace showing too. He pushed a little harder and the huge mushroom cap was half way in and again Paxton stopped. He was actually feeling my pain this time. I couldn't let this beautiful thoughtful boy who apparently loved me suffer the pain of losing his ass cherry twice in one night.

"Fuck it!" I yelled pushing against the assault with all my might and at the same time I got my hands under the fold of his knees, gripped, launched myself forward and impaled my ass on his cock in one swift motion. He was in!

I was feeling pleasantly full. The burn was still very much present but subsiding. He smiled, a look of relief on his face. I returned the same look to him. He started pistoning in all the way and pulling almost out before shoving back in me. My prostate was being massaged by his vein-mapped cock, both when it slid in and again on the way out. Something was changing though. I could feel his cock sensations just like it was me fucking me and I could tell that he was feeling what it felt like to be filled and fucked by his dick. This was amazing. I never heard any of the boys in the 'know' talk about that when bragging about the girls they fucked.

Because we were each feeling what was happening to us as well as what the other was feeling, we knew just how to move and what angle to have. It was a complete double your pleasure experience. Because we were so new at this it was way too intense and I felt Paxton's orgasm building up. I could also feel my dick getting ready to spurt another load and I wasn't even being touched. Soon it happened, we both began to moan loudly and in unison, as we felt our own and each other's orgasm simultaneously. Sperm was flying out of me, some hitting my chest, some my face and mouth, one thick pearlescent string after the other.

I felt a pop as Paxton repeatedly tightened his narrow muscular glutes, trying to get deeper into me each time he ejaculated. We both looked at each other when reality hit. The pop was Paxton's condom busting. He had filled me with his sperm. I could feel the heat of it deep in my gut and now I could feel it gushing out around his dick as it globbed onto the bed. We couldn't do anything about it now.

"Sorry," Paxton thought to me, and I just shrugged.

He kissed me deeply while still buried in me and I could feel the little spasms from his manhood. Using his arms on each side of me to push up he bent his head and licked my sperm from my chest, face and lips. Then he kissed me sharing his bittersweet find with me. Eventually he was up on his knees still between my legs with Paxton Jr. (as I had dubbed his cock) still in me. I looked down to where we were joined and was still amazed by the contrast of our dick hair. Both his and mine gleamed from our shared sweat.

"Ready?" He thought to me and put his fingers at the base of his penis to hold the remnants of the rubber in place. He pulled slowly from me, the cockhead making a wet sound as it exited my hole. He smiled holding up the tattered rubber, satisfied that none had been left in me.

"Paxton, I never thought I would say this. But this gay sex thing was in two words FUCKING AWESOME! I guess I'm a queer for real and never even knew it." I said to him.

"You are not queer. You are who you are. Just as I am who I am. Just as all the brothers in this house are. If you want to take it a step further and go global so is every gay man in the world. Except in our case our whole species is this way, the men and the women. Don't ask. It will be explained." He laughed at my look of disbelief concerning the species comment.

"I have to ask, Paxton. Why was I feeling what you were feeling when you fucked me?" I asked him with all sincerity.

"Jeff it's what I've been trying to tell you,. We are now linked. Forever! No matter where in the world each of us is we will feel the other's pleasure and pain. Though FYI, we usually don't stray too far from each other except when absolutely necessary." Paxton told me this just as easily as he had told me everything else this night and I could feel that he was being totally straight with me (no pun intended).

"But that wasn't your thought voice I heard a few times giving me advice. So what was that? My super-conscious coming to my rescue?" I asked jokingly.

"Oh don't be silly Jeff. That was my father."

"Your father knew what we were doing?" I was mortified. That is why the voice sounded somewhat familiar. "Your dad was in my fucking head when I was saying and doing all that stuff with you? Why didn't you tell me? Why was he here? You people are freaks! I almost wish I had stayed in Middletown and gone to a junior college." I couldn't believe I just said that (note the keyword was 'almost wish'). But I was beside myself with embarrassment.

Not only had I just lost my virginity, but also I had lost it fucking a boy. I had sex that I spent my whole life being taught was wrong, unnatural, and I had really enjoyed it. Very calmly Paxton answered me in his deep audible voice.

"Jeff it's no big deal. Do you think I knew how to do all that stuff? I'm only nineteen, a year older than you. It was my first time too. I wanted it to be very special and to hurt as little as possible. If we had gone at it blindly not only would I have fumbled it all up but also it would have been over way too soon. I might even have caused you to suppress your feelings longer than you already have."

"But how will I be able to face your father again? " I was already planning my escape. Then I had yet another embarrassing thought. "Does that mean he is linked to us like we are to each other? I mean for the last hour has he been able to feel you and me physically just like we were feeling both of us as the same time?"

Paxton looked at me like I was mentally challenged, but then I felt him realize that I was simply new at understanding what he had probably been taught since he was a child.

"Yes he is linked to me. I am his son. Out of paternal courtesy, if you will, he blocked feeling what I felt when I penetrated you. He understood the importance of that being an intimate moment shared by just the two of us. He was present after you penetrated me so that he felt you just as if it was him you were kissing and fucking. Before you judge him just be aware that he had a very sentimental reason for doing that."

"I'll just bet he did. Like being a horny old letch trying to relive his youth vicariously through his son's cock!" Sarcasm is not my strong suit and I never thought it very becoming. Plus old letch was hardly a description of the gorgeously handsome Mr. Vanderseer. I immediately shot an apology into Paxton's mind. He smiled and thought to me his understanding.

"Come on handsome or we're going miss everything that I been rushing us toward all evening." Paxton winked at me and picked up my briefs from the floor and tossed them to me. We started getting dressed in silence. What a strange night!

After we got dressed, Paxton took me by the hand and led me through the double doors I had noticed in the bedroom earlier and out onto a large balcony. The night was turning quite cool but in the center of the outdoor furniture grouping was a circular firebox with nice hot flames licking at the chill fall night. It was actually quite comfortable. Paxton, still holding my hand, indicated that we should sit together on the cushioned wicker couch.

"So what happens now? I thought we had a timeframe to keep." I chided him as he put his arm around my shoulders.

"We did have. But nothing we do is written in stone. We have found that long-term survival depends largely on being flexible. It is especially important in a world as barbaric as this one. Anyway this is one of those times. While we were dressing, my father and I had a discussion. I think that rather than proceed to the lady's parlor, like we would normally do, followed by going to the tribal Father's party where much would be explained, the format should be changed. Father agrees with me. Because of the way you have been raised, the introduction to the ladies would only confuse you more. So we are going to put that last. You will skip the tribal Father's meeting until another time. My father is on his way here now and is in fact walking down the hallway to the room as we speak."

I really hadn't psyched myself up enough yet to meet Paxton's father again. No more had I thought that thought than Mr. Vanderseer joined us on the balcony. I am sure my face was glowing as red as the embers in the fire and my penis had retreated to a miniscule version of itself. Traitor! I thought to it. Both Paxton and his father chuckled. I've got to watch what I think around these guys.

Paxton and I stood up as Mr. Vanderseer approached us. He smiled and patted his son on the back and then leaned forward and kissed his forehead. I was astounded seeing them standing together how very much they resembled each other. Both were beautiful. Their profiles were almost identical. Mr. Vanderseer appeared a few years older than his son and his dark hair was in a business cut contrasting to Paxton's long silky hair, as befitted a student. Their mutual love and respect for each other was very apparent. Mr. Vanderseer then turned his attention to me. Reaching out both arms he brought me into a firm hug and kissed my forehead.

"Welcome to our family Jeff." He said warmly in his deep rich voice. "I understand you and Paxton have quickly become friends tonight." Well that was an unexpected understatement. Like he should know.

"Well th-th-thankyou Mr. Vanderseer." I stuttered feeling like a kid who just got caught playing with himself.

I didn't know if thank you was the appropriate answer to the man who had just instructed me on how to fuck his son. Paxton and I sat back down on the couch. I attempted to sit some inches from him but when I did Paxton just moved over until our thighs and shoulders were touching. There was a little electricity when he did that but my dick was still in hiding. Mr. Vanderseer sat in a large chair directly across from us.

"Jeff, you have had more thrown at you tonight than most boys will experience during their lifetime. I am aware of all the questions you have been asking Paxton to answer. Some he had been told not to answer and others he did not know the answer. I am going to just start talking. I would appreciate it if you would give me the courtesy of just listening. Some of the facts surrounding you and us are going to be pretty unbelievable. However, trust me, we have no reason to ever lie to you about anything. This evening is just the beginning of your awakening to who you really are. The mind share that you and Paxton have is small compared to what lies ahead for you. Did you not notice that once Paxton spoke to you telepathically that you were immediately able to start doing it with ease. You can do that because we are a million years ahead of the human race on the evolutionary scale. You are not quite as far along as most of the boys in Omega Omega Omega simply because you were raised by a human family and had no one to awaken the kernels of your potential. Humans raised none of the other boys here, but many have not fraternized with their own kind, other than their parents, while growing up. To do so would have put our race at risk. If the children were brought up in groups their curiosity and immaturity would have brought out traits that would have made them suspect to humans and our work here would be at an end. Also, there are those who would destroy us out of fear. That is what happened to your birth parents." He had really gotten my attention on that one.

"Did you know my father and mother?" I had to ask.

"Yes. Please let me continue. But we are at a good place for me to tell you about your parents."

"Your father was one of the most respected design engineers in the world. Your mother was a brilliant scientist whose expertise was chemical physics. As scientists, they knew how close to the end of civilization the earth is. Ecologically this planet is a house of cards and it is just about to start coming down. For six hundred years our kind has tried to save mankind from itself. We have tried to sway things politically; we have introduced technology to save time and energy, but to no avail. After many meetings and years of study, your father had been granted permission to share some of our technology with mankind. He did all the right things according to the laws of this land. He applied for and was granted a patent for his technology. He was going to introduce the means of making homes and transportation almost completely independent of outside energy sources. Every car, plane, train, house would have a nearly inexhaustible and safe energy supply. The Fathers realized that this would plummet the world into turmoil for many years and could crash many world economies. There would be no need for petroleum or coal based energy of any kind. Yes it would be devastating but the world would survive and adjust and ideally mankind could devote itself to reducing world population, increasing food production without destroying the forests and soils, cleaning the environment from generations of abuse, and replenishing the oceans and lakes, to the extent possible. The biggest factor would be the reduction in population growth. There would no longer be the need for wars over petroleum, because it largely would not be needed. The list of benefits after the "pain" goes on and on. Our own species did this hundreds of thousands of years ago.

Once the governments and corporations of the world quit laughing at your father and realized the technology was authentic, they had your father and mother murdered. Their greed for power and profit outweighed their love for human kind. While investigating your parents for the source of his knowledge they almost stumbled onto our kind. They could not quite put their finger on us and in fact most of their employers thought they were crazy. Some, however, believed that your father and mother were different and since they had prematurely killed them they turned their attention to you. They wanted to study you, raise you quarantined from the world. We found this out and we had to act quickly. We substituted a recently deceased child for you. The room where a state-appointed foster couple housed you was set on fire. That body was incinerated. The foster family was unharmed and you were presumed dead. We moved you from your home in California to Ohio where we found you the family who adopted you and raised you as their own. It was for your safety. But I have been watching you grow and following you since. I appealed to the Fathers to take possession of you but was persuaded it best to leave things as they were until now." Mr. Vanderseer stopped at this point and indicated I could speak.

"What about my uncle. Did they kill him too?" I asked. I knew my eyes were red as tears formed despite my efforts to stop them. Sadness about what my life would have been like if my dad had raised me and I also felt anger that a greedy society had deprived me of my birthright. Paxton took my hand and squeezed. I am with you he thought to me.

"You never had an uncle, Jeff. Our species lives for a much longer time than earthlings and we began population control millenia ago. We never have but one son and one daughter. In rare instances there is permission granted for three possibly four children if unnatural deaths cause an imbalance in our population. But those pairings are carefully selected."

"But I'm sure I remember an uncle. I couldn't have been over three but it seems he was with us really a lot." I pressed.

"That was me. I was your father's mate. Just as you are Paxton's mate now." Mr. Vanderseer stated this simply but I recognized sadness in his voice.

"Wait a minute! Are you saying my dad was queer too?" I realized this was a stupid question since I had already been told that our whole race was this way. It was just kind of hard for me to digest after everything I had been taught about the evils of homosexuality.

"I loved your father very much Jeff. We linked when we were the same age as you and Paxton. In fact we made love in this same room and bed about seventy-five years ago. We enjoyed each other, just as the two of you will do, for many years before we bred with your mothers. That is why, and I hope you will forgive me, that I had to be mentally present in my son when you mated with him tonight. I had to relive one more time how your father's cock felt when he was in me. Each male and each female of our species is almost identical to their father or mother. Every move you made in me and every touch you gave Paxton was just like your father would have done. I was allowed to revisit a realm of very happy memories. We link for life and I have not been with a man since the death of your father nor will I ever be. I just wanted to feel him moving in me again. But I promise that without your permission I will never invade your intimacy with my son again." I didn't say anything.

"You are curious about the women. I don't mean to make it sound without feeling, this mating thing. The fact is, we love our female counterpart very much and they love us. But unlike most humans, ours is more of a race continuance relationship. That is, the heterosexual matings we have are like consolidating a business agreement. With our technology we could do it artificially, but physical union of the child's parents is a time-honored tradition. It is a concept that is difficult to explain. We are each a giver. We give each other a son and a daughter. The fathers raises his son and the mothers her daughter. We are not out of each other's life. We care for each other very much as the parent of our child and would give our life for the other if the need arose. But our species evolved as a homosexual society. We both contribute equally to society with no gender-based prejudices. The woman who will be the mother of your children is waiting to meet you. You will find that you are very compatible in your likes and dislikes. Just like you, she has a mate she has linked with for life. In some cases, depending on the career chosen by the individual it is necessary for the man and woman to function as a couple. The political life is a good example of this. This society seems to think that to be well rounded the political leaders must have a consort of the opposite sex. So our members sacrifice for a time and provide this image, but the link mate is never far away. In fact, Paxton will be in bed with you when you mate for your child's conception, as you will be with him for his mating.

I lay with your father when he mated for you. Years from now when you have finished your work here you will go to our home world where you will be welcomed and live as a couple. I will not have that opportunity. I will be alone but I will have the two of you, my offspring and the son of my link-mate.

You will learn more as time goes by. The two of you will be faced with a lot as this world crumbles into chaos in the not too distant future. Hopefully we all three will survive it. There will be war, starvation, and general mayhem. We extended our hand and it resulted in the death of the man I loved. That hand will not be extended again. Our function will be to watch humanity as we have in the past. The race mentality of humankind is too greedy. There is a theory that if they relapse into another stone age and we can direct their growth, they may have a productive future. There will be no religion and other superstitions so that they won't be ruled by fear and we will stress scientific fact and humanity. We will see. Do you have any further questions Jeff Hanover?"

I sat staring and Mr. Vanderseer for a full minute without speaking. I was just trying to absorb what had been shared with me. Then I said aloud, "Jeff Hanover? As in Hanover House?"

"Told you that cost was not a problem." Paxton spoke this time. "The Hanover wealth was placed into trusts all over the world where it would be safe until you reached majority. In other words, I have landed one rich husband."

"I don't think I've done too badly either." I countered him. Leaning over I kissed him on the lips. This time I was not self-conscious in front of the elder Mr. Vanderseer. I knew that as the son of his life mate, I was a welcome addition to his clan.

"I do have one more question Sir," I directed to Paxton's father, who raised his eyebrows waiting for me to ask.

"If we are from some distant world, why do we look just like humans?" I couldn't help but ask.

"Jeff, you have asked the one question that I cannot answer. We don't know. We have a theory that a race of super intelligent beings traveled the universe and planted life on many planets. They may still be doing it. The universe is vast and seemingly without end. Whoever they were or are they have not made us privy to their reasoning. Were we an experiment whose actions are even now being recorded or did they know the end result as they fostered life in the galaxies? In the worlds we know of, evolving intelligent life all appear in our form. What makes us different? The most accepted theory is that race mentality is a result of the world in which life was placed. That is, just as an earth child may grow up to be the product of his environment, so are a world's civilizations a product of that planet. If earthlings had been placed in a world with the opportunities of our home planet they may have turned out like us. This concept makes sense to most of us. Will we ever know for sure? Perhaps."

Question and answer time apparently over, Mr. Vanderseer smiled and we all stood up and reentered the bedroom.

"If there are no more questions, at least for the time being, we need to go to the ladies parlor and meet your mother-mate. After that I am sure that you two boys will want to come up here and continue getting to "know" each other."

On that truly happy thought, we entered the wide hallway. Mr. Vanderseer put his arms around each of our shoulders and we strode down the hall to a new future.

The End.

About the Author

Stefan Pride lives with his partner and two dogs in Houston. Stefan enjoys writing male/male erotica in his spare time. Avid travelers, Stefan and his partner can be found visiting Europe, hiking in the Andes, or wherever their wanderlust takes them. Stefan would love to hear from his readers. If you are interested in hearing more about the Jeff and Paxton saga please let him know. Or if you have any fantasies you would like to see in book form shoot him an idea. You can email him at StefanPride@yahoo.com. He also is working on a website and blog. As of this writing it is still under construction but keep checking Stefanpride.com. An avid history buff, Stefan's first full-length novel, Before Eternity Volume One, is a gay historical fiction based on Alexander the Great and his lifelong lover, the handsome Hephaestion but with a bizarre twist. Before Eternity, Volume One will be available in 2011.

Stefan began writing for fun when just in junior high. He would write humorous stories involving his teachers. That ended, when one of his stories was confiscated by his science teacher, who found no humor in the fiction which told the story of the science instructor's romance with the old maid math teacher. Today, when time permits, Stefan still enjoys writing erotic fiction based on people he knows.